1913: The Year the World Changed

Dear Reader

One hundred years ago, the world was a very different place. Many of the things we now take for granted, like highways, petrol stations, zippers, crossword puzzles, air travel and items made from stainless steel, were making their first appearance.

> "1913 WAS A TIME WHEN MANY NEW IDEAS, TECHNOLOGIES AND WAYS OF DOING THINGS BEGAN TO ALTER HOW SOCIETIES AROUND THE WORLD HAD OPERATED FOR CENTURIES."

Many of the things we now think of as normal in modern-day society, like the right to vote, were also not fully available to most people. The last century has seen a complete revolution in the way we live. I hope you enjoy reading about life a hundred years ago – and I hope, like me, you'll wonder how much more life will change in the next hundred years!

John Parsons

NELSON
A Cengage Company

Contents

1913: The Year the World Changed

1 **A World on the Verge of Change** page 4

After 1913, the ways people lived, worked and thought would never be the same.

2 **The Struggle for Equality** page 8

Dissatisfaction with the way people had been governed was about to come to a head.

3 **The End of the Empires** page 14

The royal families that ruled vast empires were soon to be threatened by monumental upheavals.

4 **The Beginnings of Modern Transport** page 20

With advances in transport, the world was on the verge of seeming a lot smaller.

5 **An Artistic Revolution** page 26

New ideas about how people could express themselves were taking hold.

TEXT TYPE Response

Index and Glossary page 32

1 A World on the Verge of Change

1913

In 1913, an exhibition of modern art, called the Armory Show, was held in New York, USA. For many people, this was the first opportunity for them to see some new styles of art that were becoming popular in Europe at that time. Here is what one reviewer, writing in a New York newspaper, had to say about the modern works on display, from art movements such as cubism, impressionism and futurism, and renowned artists such as Picasso, Van Gogh, Gauguin and Cézanne.

"If you tied a paint brush to a cow's tail and then placed her in front of a canvas where flies could worry her, you would have a futurist painting. The best I can say about the exhibition is that it would have been twice as bad if there had been twice as many pictures."

the Armoury Show catalogue

the Cubist style of modern art

Another reviewer disliked the paintings so much that he declared "the only thing I enjoyed was the beautiful brickwork in the walls of the gallery".

Today, artworks by these same artists are highly valued. In the first years of the twenty-first century, paintings by Cézanne have reached staggering prices of up to $250 million. Picasso's artworks have sold for as much as $124 million. The record price for a Van Gogh painting was over $82 million. The world of art, as with much of the world around us, has changed enormously in the last 100 years. (You can find out more about how people felt about modern art in 1913 in Chapter 5: An Artistic Revolution on page 26.)

Pablo Picasso (1881–1973) in his studio (right). Picasso was born in Spain, but divided his time between Barcelona and Paris. He was a prolific artist who created paintings, sculpture, ceramics and drawings.

In many ways, 1913 was the year before the world started to change rapidly. It was a time when many new ideas, technologies and ways of doing things began to alter how societies around the world had operated for centuries. 1913 was also the year before World War I started. World War I was a period of conflict that resulted in great changes in society, vast political upheavals, rapid technological advances and a change in expectations from many people throughout the world. Although changes had been occurring before that year, after 1913, the world as most people knew it would never be the same.

Many of the things that we take for granted 100 years later appeared for the first time in 1913. Novel inventions, such as the zipper, were developed. A new type of puzzle, the crossword, first appeared in a magazine in the USA. Stainless steel, which most of us use every day, was first created in England. Up until 1913, post offices in the UK had only delivered letters – but, in 1913, it was decided that delivering parcels might also be a good idea. As a novelty, confectionary manufacturers hit upon the idea of including a small toy in each packet of sweets. And, for the first time, a government decided that a new proposal, called income tax, would be a good way to raise money. In 1913, in the USA, the first income tax was set at a rate of 1% of the income that workers there earned.

Hmm. 13 down. A three-letter word describing how the government turns my money into their money. I'd better go and see my accountant.

I just hope my zipper stays done up. It looks too easy to be true!

1913

For centuries, the ways people lived their lives had changed very slowly. But in the single century after 1913, the world and its peoples lived through more rapid changes than had ever been experienced before.

THE CROSSWORD PUZZLE

In 1913 a journalist, Arthur Wynne, published what he called a "word-cross" puzzle in a magazine called *New York World*. Some people liked the puzzles, but many did not. One newspaper reporter said crossword puzzles were a waste of time spent "in the utterly futile finding of words, the letters of which will fit into a prearranged pattern, more or less complex. This is not a game at all." Others declared that they were just a fad, and predicted they would disappear within a few months.

THE ZIPPER

In 1913, the zipper was invented by a Swede, Gideon Sundback, who was working as an engineer in an American factory. He called his invention the "Hookless Fastener Number One". His zipper-making machine could produce about 60 metres of zipper per day. Zippers were first used to zip up a new kind of rubber gumboot. It wasn't until 10 years later that the term "zipper" was coined – and it took 20 years for people to realise they would be useful on clothes! They became most popular on children's clothes, as many young children had difficulty learning how to do up buttons!

STAINLESS STEEL

Stainless steel, which does not rust or corrode like ordinary steel, was first made by Harry Brearly in August 1913. He added chromium and carbon in varying amounts to ordinary steel, and discovered that this mix resulted in a durable steel that did not tarnish. Brearly had been brought up in Sheffield, an area of England that had been famous for making cutlery since the 1600s. At the time, he was trying to make a type of steel that could be used in gun barrels, but he immediately realised how useful his new product would be for making knives, forks and other kitchen utensils. Brearly's discovery had such an impact on the cutlery-making industry that, when he died in 1948, he was buried in Sheffield Cathedral.

2 The Struggle for Equality

An **Equal** Say

"Give us bread and roses" was a catch-cry of the suffragette movement. It meant that to flourish, women needed not only essentials, like bread, but also to be valued and appreciated for their contribution to society.

Nineteen thirteen was an important year in the struggle for equality between men and women. For centuries, in every country that held elections, only men had been allowed to vote. But from the early 1800s, increasing numbers of women were demanding that they, too, should have an equal say in how their governments were chosen. The right to vote was called "suffrage", and those women who were involved in the movement to give women a vote were called "suffragettes".

suffragettes in 1913

KING HENRY VI OF ENGLAND

In England, men were first given the right to vote in 1492. But King Henry VI decided that only men who owned property worth more than 40 shillings were eligible. In those days, that was an enormous amount of money, so few men were actually entitled to vote. King Henry VI's decision lasted with few amendments for 340 years until 1832, when men who lived in houses worth more than 10 pounds were also allowed to vote. This still meant 6 out of 7 men in England were not able to vote. It wasn't until 1918 that all English men were given the right to vote.

King Henry VI (1421–1471) restricted the voting rights of Englishmen to the very wealthy.

In 1893, New Zealand became the first country in the world to allow women to vote. The state of South Australia followed in 1894, becoming the first in Australia to give men and women equal voting rights. Despite these changes, in 1913 most countries around the world still denied women a say when it came to choosing governments.

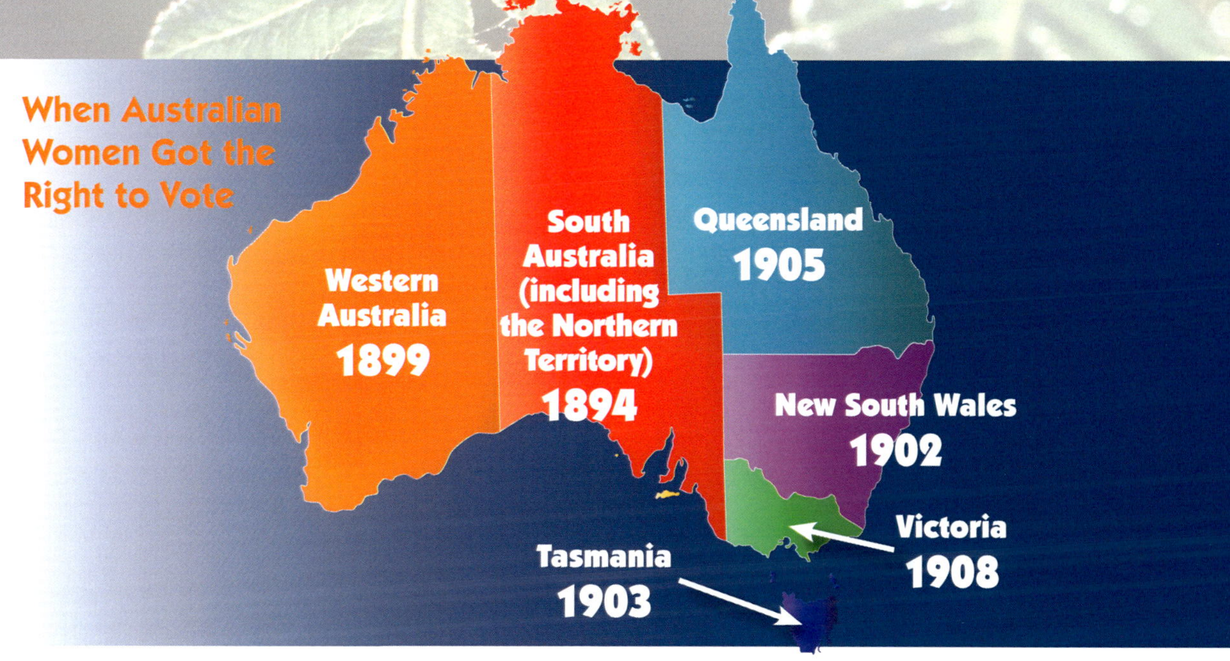

VOTING RIGHTS FOR ALL AUSTRALIANS

In the mid-nineteenth century, Victoria, New South Wales, Tasmania and South Australia gave voting rights to all male British subjects over 21. As Indigenous Australian males were also British subjects, they were entitled to vote. However, few Indigenous Australians were informed about their rights under British law, so many did not know they were entitled to vote.

In 1894, South Australia's decision to give men and women equal voting rights was a progressive move. Furthermore, because every woman was entitled to vote, this meant that Indigenous Australian women were, for the first time, also entitled to vote.

Years of misunderstandings and, in some cases, deliberate obstruction by people in power, around Indigenous Australians' voting rights followed, however.

Later, South Australia's constitution, and its insistence that all South Australian men and women be allowed to vote in federal elections, became an important part of the legal battle to ensure that all Indigenous Australians understood their voting rights and were able to exercise them freely and fully throughout Australia.

In the USA, in March 1913, a group of women paraded in front of the White House holding placards and demanding they be allowed to vote. In April 1913, there were several general strikes in Belgium, where workers refused to go to work in support of voting rights for women. In June, demonstrations in the Netherlands attracted thousands of protesters, all demanding that women be given the vote.

the program of events for the 1913 suffragette procession in the USA (below)

But it was in Britain, where women had been trying to get the vote for almost a century, that patience was running out amongst the suffragettes. Some suffragette groups staged violent protests. Throughout 1913, windows in shops and government buildings were smashed by protesters. Some buildings were set on fire. A few suffragettes deliberately assaulted members of the police so that they would be arrested. Once they were arrested and put in prison, these women would go on a hunger strike, refusing to eat until they became extremely ill. In 1913, the British government, which didn't want to be held responsible for protesters starving themselves to death, passed a law that came to be known as the "Cat and Mouse" law. Women on hunger strikes were left to starve until they almost died, and then they were released from prison to recover. As soon as they became healthy again, they were re-arrested and thrown back in jail.

A British suffragette campaigns on a London street.

UNIVERSAL SUFFRAGE

In 1889, a group of settlers and indigenous people in a province of Vanuatu declared independence. This new country was named Franceville. Everybody in Franceville, regardless of ethnicity or gender, was entitled to vote, and Franceville therefore became the first self-governing country in the world to grant "universal suffrage", or votes for everyone. Unfortunately, the British and French authorities that governed the rest of Vanuatu resisted the efforts of the people in Franceville, and within two years, it had been forced to give up its independence.

Emmeline Pankhurst, one of England's most militant suffragettes, travelled to the USA in 1913 to give a speech in which she declared that the British government would have to choose between giving women "freedom or death". She was arrested that year; one of eight times that she was put in prison for her beliefs.

Emmeline Pankhurst (above and right) was arrested several times for advocating violence to achieve the aims of the suffragette movement. She died in 1928, the year that women eventually got full voting rights in the UK.

But one of the most shocking events in 1913 occurred at a famous horse race called the Epsom Derby. A suffragette called Emily Davison decided that a good way to protest would be to stop one of the races. She chose one in which King George V had a horse running. As the horses approached, she ran onto the track calling "votes for women". Unfortunately, the horses were travelling too fast to avoid her. Emily was knocked over by the king's horse, and died of her injuries four days later*.

* Read more about Emily Davison in the Nelson Literacy Directions 6 big book, *The Kids' Guide to Government.*

A FIRST-HAND ACCOUNT OF EMILY DAVISON'S PROTEST, 1913

"I was watching the horses approaching the corner, when I noticed a figure bob under the rails on the opposite side to which I was standing. The horses were thundering down the course at a great pace bunched up against the rail. It was obviously her intention to stop the race. Misjudging the pace of the horses, she missed the first four or five. They dashed by just as she was emerging from the rails. With great calmness she walked in front of the next group of horses.

"The first missed her, but the second, Anmer, came right into her, and catching her with his shoulders, knocked her with terrific force to the ground while the crowd stood spellbound. The woman rolled over two or three times, and lay unconscious. She was thrown almost on her face. Anmer fell after striking the woman, pitching Jones, the jockey, clear over its head. Fortunately, Anmer fell clear of the woman, and the horses following swerved by the woman, the jockey and the fallen horse."

Anonymous, 1913

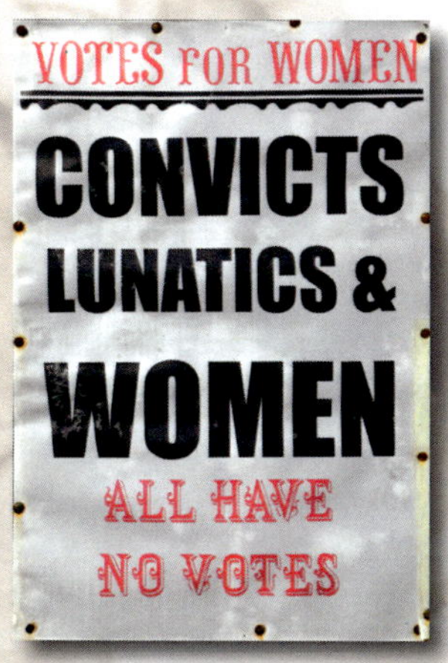

The struggle for equal voting rights was at its most passionate in 1913, and protests continued in Britain, Europe and many other countries throughout the year. However, despite the protests, women in Britain had to wait another 15 years, until 1928, before they were given the same voting rights as men.

3 The End of the Empires

Monarchies and Colonies

In 1913, there were far fewer independent countries than there are now. Many European countries were ruled by monarchies, and many of these countries had seized or created colonies across the world to build empires – groups of countries ruled by a single government or person, usually a monarch. Some of the most powerful European monarchies and their empires were the British Empire, the German Empire, the Austro-Hungarian Empire and the Russian Empire. Italy, Portugal and the Netherlands also had empires. France, while it no longer had a monarchy, governed vast colonies across the world. At the edge of Europe, the Ottoman Empire ruled much of northeast Africa and the Middle East.

King George V, ruler of the British empire (left), and his family at Buckingham Palace, painted by Sir John Lavery in 1913.

EMPERORS, EMPIRES AND COLONIES IN 1913

KING GEORGE V, BRITISH EMPIRE

King George V was ruler of the British Empire, which encompassed the UK, Ireland, Australia, New Zealand, Canada, much of southern and eastern Africa, the Middle East, India and other parts of Asia and the South Pacific.

KAISER WILHELM II, GERMAN EMPIRE

Kaiser Wilhelm II was ruler of the German Empire, which encompassed Germany, Papua New Guinea, Samoa, Namibia, Cameroon, Tanzania and parts of China and the north Pacific.

EMPEROR FRANZ JOSEPH I, AUSTRO-HUNGARIAN EMPIRE

Emperor Franz Joseph I was ruler of the Austro-Hungarian Empire, which encompassed Austria, Hungary, Bosnia and Herzegovina, Croatia, Czech Republic, Slovakia, Slovenia, Serbia, Romania, and parts of Poland and the Ukraine.

CZAR NICHOLAS II, RUSSIAN EMPIRE

Czar Nicholas II was ruler of the Russian Empire, which encompassed Russia, Ukraine, Belarus, Moldova, Finland, Armenia, Azerbaijan, Georgia, Kazakhstan, Kyrgyzstan, Tajikistan, Turkmenistan, Uzbekistan, most of Lithuania, Estonia and Latvia, as well as much of Poland and parts of Turkey.

SULTAN MEHMED V, OTTOMAN EMPIRE

Sultan Mehmed V was ruler of the Ottoman Empire, which encompassed Turkey, Egypt, Sudan, Saudi Arabia, and much of the Middle East.

The European empires, which were ruled by people who were related to each other, set up complicated agreements and alliances between one another. If one went to war, the others promised to help. The web of alliances that existed in 1913 would have terrible consequences one year later, when the heir to the throne of the Austro-Hungarian Empire, Archduke Franz Ferdinand, was killed in Sarajevo, which at that time was part of the empire. The world was plunged into the First World War.

The British, Russian and French empires ended up fighting against the German, Austro-Hungarian and Ottoman empires. At the end of the war, the German, Austro-Hungarian, Russian and Ottoman empires had all collapsed, and some estimates say over 15 million people were dead. Nineteen thirteen marked the last year when the empires that had governed much of Europe for centuries held sway.

Many countries involved in World War I gained a new sense of nationhood during the conflict. The independence of Australian and New Zealand troops (seen here landing at Gallipoli in 1915) sometimes brought them into conflict with their British commanders.

A FAMILY ARGUMENT

King George V was a first cousin to both Kaiser Wilhelm II and Czar Nicholas II, and all were distant cousins of Emperor Franz Joseph I.

Kaiser Frederick III *married* Princess Victoria → **Kaiser Wilhelm II**

Princess Victoria *sister of* King Edward VII

King Edward VII *married* Queen Alexandra → **King George V**

Queen Alexandra *sister of* Empress Maria

Empress Maria *married* Czar Alexander III → **Czar Nicholas II**

In other parts of the world, 1913 also marked the end of an era for major empires. In China, the last emperor of the Qing dynasty, the 7-year-old Pu-Yi, was stripped of his royal status. His aunt, Longyu, the last Chinese empress, died. Two thousand years of imperial rule in China was over. In 1913, the first ever Chinese parliament was opened in Beijing.

Emperor Pu-Yi, aged 3, (on the right), known as the "ruler of 430 million souls" stands next to his father, Prince Chun, who is holding Pu-Yi's younger brother.

a painting of Empress Longyu

THE END OF THE QING DYNASTY

Pu-Yi's father, together with his aunt, Empress Longyu, ruled China until 1912, when the country had a revolution and became a republic. In 1949, the Chinese government was overthrown by communists led by Mao Zedong. Pu-Yi, who was born in 1906 and died in 1967, lived through many of the most momentous changes to occur in Chinese society. He started life as a royal, was made to work as a gardener, and ended his life as a book editor.

A NEW CAPITAL FOR AUSTRALIA

"I have planned a city that is not like any other in the world. I have planned it not in a way that I expected any government authorities in the world would accept. I have planned an ideal city – a city that meets my ideal of the city of the future."

Walter Burley Griffin

In 1913, work on Australia's new capital city began. A capital city was to be an important symbol of Australia's growing independence from Great Britain. Since Federation in 1901, both Melbourne and Sydney had been vying to be Australia's capital, but politicians from those cities could not agree on which was more suitable. Eventually, it was decided that a new neutral territory (present-day Australian Capital Territory, or ACT) should be set up and the capital established there. A competition to design the new capital city was held and, in 1911, a design by Walter Burley Griffin and Marion Mahony Griffin was chosen.

In February, the first survey pegs were driven in to mark the layout of the new city. On 12 March, at Kurrajong Hill, the wife of the governor-general, Lady Denman, officially gave the new city its name: Canberra. A foundation stone was laid, and Kurrajong Hill is now the site of Parliament House. Walter Burley Griffin commenced work building the new city*.

Canberra's naming ceremony

building work commences in Canberra

* Read more about Canberra and Parliament House in the NLD 6 big book, *The Kids' Guide to Government*.

NON-VIOLENCE

Mohandas Gandhi (1869–1948)

In South Africa in 1913, an Indian lawyer named Mohandas Gandhi led a number of protests against the discrimination of non-Europeans by British rulers. Gandhi had been born in India but moved to South Africa following his education in Britain. During the 20 years he spent in South Africa, Gandhi developed his philosophy of peaceful protest – a philosophy that later become known as non-violence. He believed that change could best be brought about not by using violence, but by peacefully disobeying unfair laws. In 1913, he was arrested three times and thrown in jail for leading protests that encouraged Indians in South Africa to disobey British laws.

During 1913, Gandhi realised that, while the Indians in South Africa faced discrimination and prejudice, the situation was far worse in India itself. The following year, in 1914, he set off back to India. His work over the next 30 years led directly to India achieving independence in 1947. Gandhi is known as the "father" of modern India.

OTHER POLITICAL "FIRSTS"

In 1913, most people got their information through newspapers. Politicians realised that people's opinions were often formed by what they read in these newspapers. Woodrow Wilson, the president of the United States of America, decided on a new and innovative way to get his views and policies across to the public. In March 1913, he decided to hold the first-ever presidential press conference. It is a tradition that continues to this day.

Woodrow Wilson (1856–1924)

4 The Beginnings of Modern Transport

THE MOVING ASSEMBLY LINE

In the early years of the twentieth century, cars were becoming more common, but they were still expensive and only wealthy people could afford them. That all changed in 1913, when an American industrialist named Henry Ford developed a moving assembly line at his car factory in Detroit. He realised that he could lower costs and increase productivity by having his workers each assemble a small part of a car on a conveyor belt, rather than having the workers move around the factory, doing many different jobs.

The idea of a moving assembly line was so successful that, instead of taking 12 hours to assemble a single car, it took only one-and-a-half. A new car rolled off Ford's innovative assembly line every 15 minutes. In fact, the lines were so efficient that they caused problems when the cars came to be painted. The only paint that would dry fast enough to cope with the numbers of cars coming off the line was black. Ford is reputed to have said that his customers could have a car any colour they liked "as long as it was black". It wasn't until fast-drying paint colours were developed in 1926 that the painters at the end of the moving assembly line could use different colours and still keep up with the cars lining up behind them!

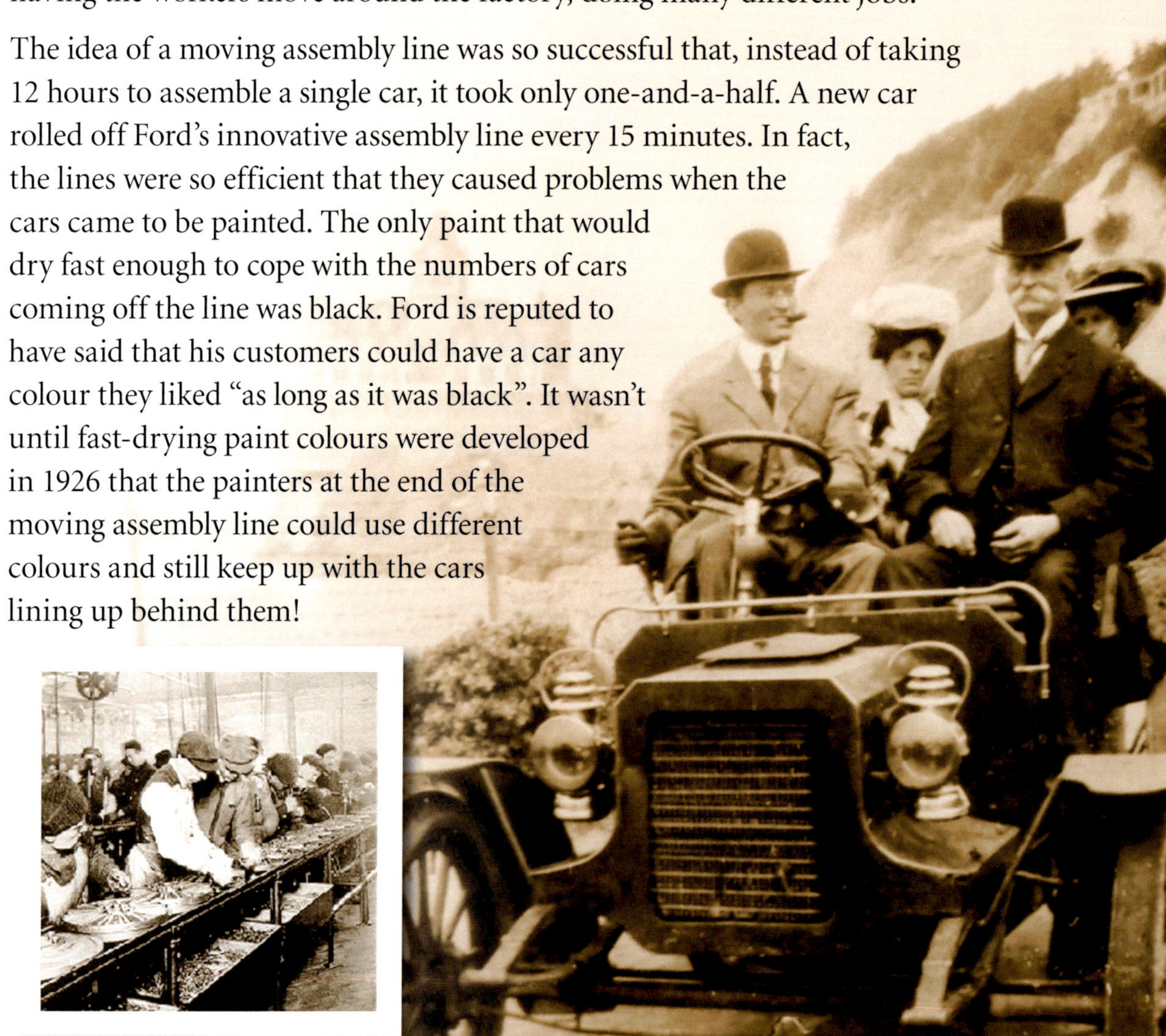

Ford assembly line workers in 1913

A family enjoys their new-found motoring freedom.

HIGHWAYS

With the increasing numbers of cars, there were more demands for better roads and better road networks. The Lincoln Highway, the USA's first paved coast-to-coast highway, was officially opened for traffic in September 1913. It runs from New York to San Francisco. Better facilities for drivers were also needed, and on 1 December 1913, the world's first drive-in petrol station was opened in Pittsburgh. From a single station in 1913, the number of petrol stations increased over the next century to a peak of 202 000 in 1994.

the Lincoln Highway (left) in 1913; an early petrol pump (right)

PUBLIC TRANSPORT

To cope with the huge number of train passengers entering and leaving Manhattan in New York, USA, the iconic Grand Central Station was opened in 1913. With 44 platforms, it is still considered the world's largest railway station, and its architecture and design are renowned throughout the world.

Workers on Grand Central Station (above right) had to excavate almost 3 million cubic metres of earth and rock from the site in the process of moving existing train lines underground. The freed-up land above ground made room for the skyscrapers that now make up the Manhattan skyline.

AIRCRAFT

The first aircraft flew in 1903 and, ten years later, aircraft development was still in its early stages. In Russia, an engineer called Igor Sikorsky built and flew the first-ever four-engined aircraft in May 1913. A French aviator, Roland Garros, became the first pilot to cross the Mediterranean Sea in a plane, flying from southern France to Tunisia in September 1913. The first aerobatic manoeuvre, a loop, was performed by a Russian pilot, Peter Nestrov. And, perhaps wisely, 1913 saw the first-ever parachute jump from an aircraft, which was done by Adolphe Pégoud in France. But the slow pace of aircraft development would change forever the following year, when World War I broke out. Both sides quickly realised the advantage of having reliable aircraft for military purposes, and the pace of aircraft development accelerated rapidly.

an early parachute jump (above); an aircraft training accident (below)

In 1913, there were only 850 pilots in Britain; but from 1914 until 1918, tens of thousands of people were trained as pilots. Incredibly, out of the 14 000 pilots killed in World War I, over 8 000 were killed in training accidents. Even with the advances in aircraft technology, it was more dangerous to learn to fly than to actually go to war!

ROLAND GARROS

Because of his expertise in flying aircraft, Roland Garros became a fighter pilot for the French Air Force in World War I. He was killed in 1918. Before the war, when he wasn't flying aircraft, Garros was a keen tennis player. While he was attending school in Paris, he would regularly go to a tennis centre in the west of Paris and, in the 1920s, it was named the *Stade de Roland Garros* in honour of the pilot. A hundred years after Garros became famous for flying across the Mediterranean Sea, the stadium that bears his name is the home of the French Open tennis tournament, which is also officially known as "Roland Garros".

Roland Garros flying (left); and in front of his aircraft (below)

In 1913, few people had even seen an aircraft, let alone flown in one. The rapid advances in technology that followed World War I meant that flying became more and more accessible for greater numbers of people. A hundred years later, the air transport industry carries around 2.75 billion passengers a year. Almost 980 million of these passengers fly internationally, while the remainder fly on domestic services. Around 36 million tonnes of international freight are flown around the world each year.

SEA TRANSPORT

The creation of the Panama Canal, which gave cargo ships a new, faster route between the Atlantic and Pacific oceans, was one of the most expensive and dangerous engineering projects ever undertaken. In 1913, it was finally opened. The last section of land was blown up, and a 33-year project that had cost thousands of lives and hundreds of millions of dollars was completed.

men working on the Panama Canal

For much of that time, it seemed that the construction of a canal through Panama was doomed. In 1880, a French company had started building a canal, but they had vastly underestimated the challenges of building such a huge canal through the jungle. Over 22 000 workers died from diseases and accidents, and the company went bankrupt after spending an incredible $287 million on work.

Construction work on the canal required enormous earthworks and heavy machinery.

The government of the USA took over the project a few years later and, despite continued hardships and challenges, the 82-kilometre canal was finished in 1913 and quickly became a vital passage for international shipping. After 1913, ships no longer had to travel around the bottom of South America and through the dangerous Strait of Magellan, and shipping times between the Atlantic and Pacific oceans were cut in half.

In the first year of operation, the Panama Canal saw around 1 000 ships pass through it. A hundred years later, almost 15 000 ships a year use the Panama Canal. Since 1913, over 820 000 ships have used this shortcut between oceans!

A cargo ship navigates the Panama Canal.

EXPENSIVE TOLLS

Ships pay a fee, or toll, to use the Panama Canal. The toll is calculated based on the weight and size of the ship, how many people are on board and a number of other factors. Cruise ships, which are large and carry thousands of passengers, can pay up to $380 000 to pass through the canal. The average toll is about $54 000. The cheapest ever toll was paid by an adventurer from the USA, Richard Halliburton, who decided to swim through the Panama Canal in 1928. He was charged 36 cents.

5 An Artisic Revolution

Moving Pictures

Along with looming social changes, 1913 was also a year marked by changing tastes in the arts and in entertainment.

At that time, Hollywood was a quiet, small municipality on the outskirts of Los Angeles, USA. A motion picture had been filmed there in 1910, and a small film company had converted a disused warehouse into a film studio in 1911. In December 1913, the first feature film made in Hollywood began filming. It was a western action movie called *The Squaw Man*. It cost $20 000 to make.

a panoramic view of the Hollywood area taken in 1913

Since its start in 1913, movie making has become a gigantic industry in Hollywood. In comparison to the amount spent making *The Squaw Man*, movie budgets now are often above $250 million – but the returns are huge, too. Hollywood's first movie made around $240 000 over a hundred years – the recent Hollywood film *Avatar* has made around $2.8 billion in only three years.

Early Hollywood movies were dramatic, silent and not in colour. It wasn't until 1927 that the first movie with sound was made and colour movie-making did not become practical until the 1930s.

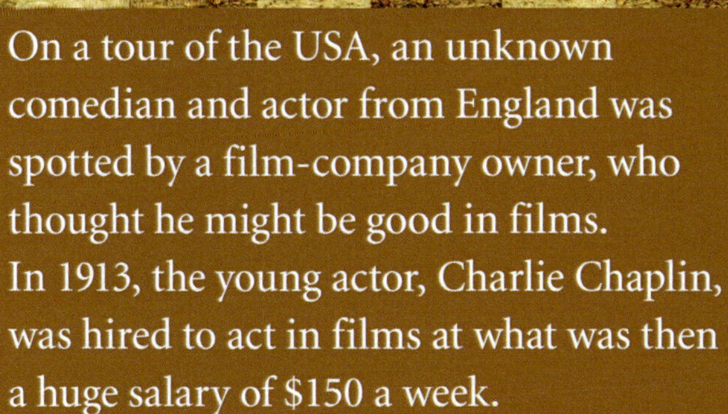

On a tour of the USA, an unknown comedian and actor from England was spotted by a film-company owner, who thought he might be good in films. In 1913, the young actor, Charlie Chaplin, was hired to act in films at what was then a huge salary of $150 a week.

Charlie Chaplin (right) was born in 1889. His silent films were full of mime, slapstick humour and visual comedy.

With the rising popularity of silent movies, some states in the USA decided that all motion pictures should be approved by the authorities before they were screened. The first censorship of films, where government authorities removed sections of movies they did not like, was approved in 1913.

THE MISSING MONA LISA

In 1913, the *Mona Lisa*, a painting by Leonardo Da Vinci, was returned to the Louvre in Paris. It had been stolen two years earlier by an employee, Vincenzo Peruggia, who had hidden the painting in a broom cupboard and walked out with it hidden under his coat.

Peruggia was an Italian who thought that da Vinci's best-known painting should be kept in Italy, where it was originally painted. After keeping the painting in his apartment for two years, Peruggia attempted to sell it to an art gallery in Florence. He was arrested and the painting was returned to France in 1913. Many Italians agreed with Peruggia's motive for stealing the painting, however, and he was only kept in jail there for six months.

Though major changes were occurring in the world of film, it was in the field of visual arts where the biggest, most controversial artistic changes were occurring in 1913. This was the year that the avant-garde art being created in Europe came to the attention of the rest of the world. In Europe, in the late 1800s, some artists decided that art should do more than just depict how objects, people and landscapes looked. They argued that, with the increasing popularity of photography, art should not be confined to being “realistic”. If people wanted to see how something looked, they could simply look at a photograph. But if people wanted to experience how an artist felt, then a new and revolutionary form of art was needed.

This new kind of art, which was called “modern art” at the time, used colour, shape and style to create a visual impression of a mood, an emotion or an event. We now know this art by the names of the major styles and techniques it used, such as cubism, impressionism, post-impressionism and abstract. Today, we are used to seeing these modern styles of art all around us, but in 1913, the idea of creating art that looked nothing like anything in the real world was hugely controversial. Nowhere was this more evident than in New York, where the first major exhibition of modern art outside Europe was opened in 1913. This exhibition became known as the Armory Show, as it was held in an old army building in the middle of New York that had been converted for use as an art gallery. The exhibition created a sensation, with reviewers and the public either loving the new art or hating it. One hundred years after the exhibition, it is interesting to read the highly critical reviews.

Over 90 000 New Yorkers visited the Armory Show in 1913.

If You Can't Understand Something, Does That Make It Good, Bad or Just Different?

TEXT TYPE
Response

A RESPONSE TO THE REVIEWS

When an exhibition of artworks by modern artists including Cézanne, Van Gogh, Gauguin and Picasso opened in New York in 1913, it was the first opportunity for many people in the USA to see the new styles of art that were being created in Europe. Art critics reviewed the exhibition in newspapers and magazines, and some wrote scathing reviews. They were familiar with seeing art that used traditional techniques to clearly and realistically depict the subject of the painting. They had never seen modern art and struggled to understand it.

Up until then, artists had made it relatively easy to identify the subject of a painting. But the subjects were not so easy to spot in the modern art exhibits. Many of the reviews expressed frustration at not being able to "see" the subject of the painting. For example, when the critics looked at a painting called *Nude Descending a Staircase*, they expected to see a woman on a staircase. Instead, they saw a collection of geometric shapes and contrasting colours.

When the critics failed to understand the paintings, they ridiculed the artists, which was unfair. The artists had never intended to paint the subject realistically. They had set out to capture an impression, a feeling, a mood or an emotion. One newspaper reviewer declared that, after seeing the exhibition, she was going to hold a modern art party where "everyone is to paint a picture, and the person who can guess what the pictures mean will get a prize. No artists allowed!" Another wrote that a painting that was supposed to show someone who was eating, actually looked like that person had just spilled a bowl of brown soup all over the canvas.

Reviewers also complained about the techniques that the painters employed. A critic in a New York newspaper protested that "a picture by Picasso, seemingly representing an object, appears made of children's blocks, cut up and put together. It is not art – it is sheer cheek!" Another wrote that Picasso's pictures "resembled a pile of red blocks after an earthquake." One reviewer, commenting on the technique of the cubists (who composed their paintings of overlapping geometric shapes) said "even a poodle could have his hour in the limelight if he were stuck all over with postage stamps and hung at eye level."

One of Gauguin's paintings had been painted in Tahiti, but he had used grey, flat colours, which the reviewers complained were not at all like the vibrant colours found in tropical islands. Gauguin had, in fact, used drab colours to express how he was feeling at the time. His painting captured his mood exactly – but the reviewers failed to understand that.

Several reviewers questioned the artists' motives. They thought the artists were merely trying to trick the people seeing the exhibition, and were trying to make money from worthless paintings. One horrified reviewer wrote that he was "absolutely skeptical as to their having any claim whatsoever to being works of art." Another wrote that modern art was worthless, "as long as the artists go on producing flatly impossible paintings."

The Armory Show of 1913 was indicative of how new or challenging ideas have often been treated throughout history. People have tended to criticise something as bad, simply because it was different or they misunderstood it. Today, modern artists such as Cézanne, Van Gogh, Gauguin and Picasso are recognised as talented, innovative leaders in the world of the arts. And a century later, most art critics would describe the artworks exhibited at the Armory Show as brilliant, evocative and inspiring. This shows that, initially, people may judge an artist's work as good or bad, based on old ideas and established views of how things should be. However, when people can appreciate something as different to anything they have seen before, they can potentially expand their understanding of the world.

Despite the critics' negative reviews, or perhaps *because* of them, over 90 000 people visited the Armory Show in 1913. Many members of the public were equally perplexed by the paintings they saw – but the exhibition was enormously successful in one important respect. It started people talking and thinking about modern art. Although they may have disagreed about it, it became firmly cemented as a new movement that could not be ignored. As more people saw the paintings, they became interested in trying to understand them. When they learned what the modern painters were really trying to capture, they realised how these artists had completely changed the direction and meaning of art. Instead of just reproducing what could be seen in the world, art had become a way of expressing the impact of the world on people's deepest feelings and emotions.

Index

modern art 4, 5, 29–31

capital city 18

cars 20, 21

cubism 4, 29

empire 14–16, 17

government 6, 8–12, 14, 17, 18, 25

inventions 6

independence 11, 16, 18, 19

protest 10–13, 19

revolution 4–5, 17, 26–31

transport 20–21, 23, 24

vote 8–12

World War 5, 16, 22, 23

zipper 6, 7

Glossary

alliances Agreements between individuals, groups or nations to cooperate for the benefit of each other

censorship The act of removing or banning material from books, films and other works because it is judged to be inappropriate for the public

cutlery Eating tools such as knives, forks and spoons

discrimination The unfair treatment of people based on a characteristic such as ethnicity, gender, age, hair colour, height, etc.

empire A group of nations ruled over by a single leader, often an emperor

futurism An art movement of the early 1900s, originating in Italy, which aimed to represent the speed and motion of machines in non-moving art forms such as painting and sculpture

militant Aggressive and uncompromising

obstruction The act of putting an obstacle in the way

placards Written or printed notices displayed in public places, often associated with protests

vying competing